For Julián, Magalí, Joaquín, Areli, & Valentino
—Y.S.M.

For kids from everywhere
—J.K.

Where Are You From?
Text copyright © 2019 by Yamile Saied Méndez
Illustrations copyright © 2019 by Jimyung Kim
All rights reserved. Printed in the United States of America.
No part of this book may be used or reproduced in any manner whatsoever without written
permission except in the case of brief quotations embodied in critical articles and reviews. For
information address HarperCollins Children's Books, a division of HarperCollins Publishers,
195 Broadway, New York, NY 10007.
www.harpercollinschildrens.com

Library of Congress Control Number: 2018943091
ISBN 978-0-06-283993-0

The artist used watercolors and digital techniques to create the digital illustrations for this book.
Typography by Erica De Chavez
20 21 22 23 PC 10 9 8 7
❖
First Edition

Where Are You From?

by **Yamile Saied Méndez** · illustrated by **Jaime Kim**

HARPER
An Imprint of HarperCollinsPublishers

Where are you from?
they ask.

Is your mom from here?

Is your dad from there?
they ask.

I'm from here, from today,
same as everyone else, I say.

No, where are you
really from? they insist.

I ask Abuelo because he knows everything,

and like me, he looks like he doesn't belong.

Abuelo thinks.
His eyes squint, like he's looking
inside his heart for an answer.

You come from the Pampas,

the open, free land, he says.

You're from the gaucho,
brave and strong.

From the brown river that cleanses and feeds the land
that gives us the grain for our bread, the milk from the cows.

You're from mountains so high
they tickle Señor Cielo's belly,

where the condor roosts his family
and the jaguar prowls the night.

But you're also from the warm, blue oceans
the copper warriors tried to tame

and the elegant palm trees
stretch their fingers to caress.

You're from hurricanes and dark storms,

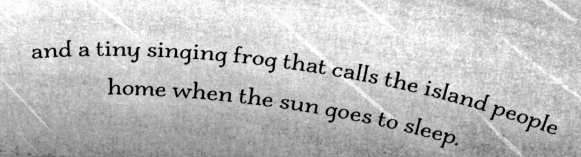

and a tiny singing frog that calls the island people
home when the sun goes to sleep.

From this land where our ancestors built a home for all,

even when they were in chains because of the color of their skin.

You're from the grandmothers who
search for their grandchildren, waiting,
always waiting in a plaza, their white
handkerchiefs wrapping the sorrow
of their thoughts.

You come from the sunshine that lights our path in this world and the rain that washes away our mistakes.

25 MAYO 1810

But, Abuelo, I ask,
where am I really from?

Abuelo laughs.
You want a place?

He points to his heart. You're from here,

from my love and the love of all those before us,

from those who dreamed of you
because of a song sung under the Southern Cross

or the words in a book written under the light of the North Star.

You?

You are from all of us.

I am.